Dedicated to my grandson
Zachary Burns who, deep in his
heart, holds love, dreams, and
an imagination strong enough to
believe that his Forever-Best
Friend Froggie is his treasured
gift to keep forever.

Acknowledgments

I want to thank my husband Jim for standing confidently beside me and supporting my writing during these last two and a half years, my son Jeffrey and daughter Jennifer for inspiring me to follow my dreams, my friends Betty Bjorkman, Ann Pearson, and my sister Sandy Murphy for sharing their skills, Meredith Lagaard and Ann Feerhusen, who provided me with constant encouragement to continue writing, my Auntie Fern who first inspired me to write, my cousin Tim Burns who persuaded me to "stick with it," my grandson Zachary's wonderful pre-school teacher, Ms. Katy from Duluth, MN, who taught me that "fewer words means more to children," my niece Kellie Murphy who spent countless hours at my side, and my many other friends who read my drafts, critiqued my work, and unfailingly gave me positive feedback. I send my blessings, my love, and my respect to you all.
You have all been my inspiration!
Pamela Christensen VanderGriend

Froggie In Lily Pad Kingdom
Published by
FROGGIE & FRIENDS, LLC
www.froggieandfriends.us/

Copyright August 2005   First Printing 2006

Story written by Pamela Christensen VanderGriend

Library of Congress Control Number: 2006906687
ISBN: 09787456-0-4 $17.95 USA   CANADA $20.95
SAN: 851-5263

First edition in print October 2006

Printed and Published in the United States of America
Corporate Graphics Commercial
Mankato, MN 56002-8800

Froggie
In
Lily Pad Kingdom

Finding His
Forever-Best Friend

Many new moons ago,
in a place called Lily Pad Kingdom,
a frog named Froggie lived peacefully with
fairies, elves, turtles, and Tinkerbells.
Among them was a fairy princess named Ida,
the Princess of Dreams to Come True
for all who lived in the kingdom.

On the second day of a bright October morning,
Froggie peered into Lily Pad Pond
and saw his reflection.

Froggie knew then,
to have a Forever-Best Friend
would be a dream come true.

But first he had to find his very own lily pad; for in
the center of the lily pad is where he would find the
dream cloud that would lead him to his
Forever-Best Friend.

A Forever-Best Friend to share play times,
happy times, learning times, scary times,
sleepy times, bad times—or even sad times
with someone special
always by his side.

Knowing the search for his dream of finding a Forever-Best Friend would soon begin, Froggie went over to the sparkling waterfall to visit Katie the Caterpillar.

But Katie the Caterpillar was not there! "Froggie,
it's me, Katie," said a beautiful butterfly.
"Princess Ida showed me the way to my dream come true,
and now I can fly.
Soon you, too, will find your dream come true."

At that moment Ida,
Princess of Dreams,
appeared at Froggie's side.
"Froggie, now is the time
for you to find
the lily pad that
holds the path to your dream.
Though this will be your hardest task,
it's the most important for the dream
you shall have.

"Now, Froggie, think about your Friend to be. At the end of your journey is where your dream will find him, as you shall see."

So Froggie began to jump and swim and swim and jump until
finally he reached the gates to Lily Pad Pond.
The vines on the gates were beautiful with colored fragrant
flowers growing on them. The gates reached so high in the sky,
he could barely see the tops of them.

Froggie jumped over the threshold, then stopped and looked.
He saw thousands of lily pads—and they all looked the same!
Now he knew finding his lily pad was going to be a difficult task.
So he quickly began to search for his lily pad.

He became so tired from jumping, leaping and searching that he needed to float in the water for only a minute in order to rest his legs and catch his breath.

Froggie rolled over in the water so his white belly faced the sky. He stretched his legs straight out with his toes peeking out of the water and wiggled them a little. His eyes were open so he could watch the clouds floating above, and his tongue was hanging out of his mouth just a teeny-tiny little bit so he could catch a mosquito if he got hungry.

As Froggie floated quietly, he saw a bright light beaming from
the far end of the pond.
"What could that be?" Froggie said to himself.
He turned right side up, careful not to take his eyes off of it.
His webbed feet barely made a ripple in the water as he
floated closer to the bright light.
The closer he got, the brighter the light became.

He saw a golden glow shining like the sun from inside a lily pad. It had a beautiful green stem that shimmered in the water clear down to where the snails and clams crawl. Its white petals appeared soft and velvety. It was the most beautiful lily pad Froggie had seen in all of Lily Pad Pond, and all he could do was stare at it.

Finally,
he squeezed his eyes shut, wishing
and hoping that the beautiful
lily pad would be his.
He yelled one big loud "Bugga-Boo"
and took a giant jump that
carried him over lily pads,
wild rice, pussy willows and ducks.
Froggie landed right smack in the
center of the beautiful
lily pad.

"Wow, this lily pad is just the way
I dreamed mine would be.
I feel as snug as a bug in a rug nestled
inside here," said Froggie.

Ida, the fairy princess, with her wings dazzling
in the sunshine, appeared at Froggie's side
and said,
"Your lily pad is your dream as seen. Now, dream
about your Friend to be."

Froggie thought about his Forever-Best Friend, but when he opened his eyes nothing had happened.

"Fiddlesticks, will my dream ever come to be?" wondered Froggie.

So............ quietly and with patience, he waited.

Froggie waited so long nestled in the center
of his lily pad that he could barely continue to keep his
eyes open. Finally he fell into a
deep
deep
sleep.
Suddenly his dream cloud began to billow up around him,
floating,
spinning and
whirling him
into a rainbow's tunnel of colors.

He was traveling so fast he
felt like a cheetah
moving like lightning
through the
rainbow
into tomorrow.
He sailed past
pelicans,
ships, loons,
and sailboats.

While he was dreaming, Froggie saw the moon at
the far end of the rainbow, as bright and round as
a full moon could be. The Northern Lights were
radiant and dancing in the night sky as the stars
sparkled like the colors of the rainbow
shining on them.

As Froggie neared
the end of the rainbow,
he began
to slow down.
Suddenly he
dropped into a
topsy-turvy
upside-down
head-over-webbed-feet
downward spiral spin,
falling,
falling,
falling,
and landed
with a soft bounce
onto a fluffy puffy
down blanket.

Froggie shook his head from side to side. He felt his heart to make sure it was still beating.

Then he looked to see where he had landed with such an ungraceful fall

W
H
E
N

He heard a soft
whispering voice
say,
"WHO ARE YOU?
And how in heavens
did you get here?"

Froggie sat motionless,
wondering
WHO
IS THAT?

"My name is Froggie,"
he said with a gulp.
"I found you with help
from Fairy Princess Ida
and my lily pad.
The fairy princess
told me to follow the
path I saw in my
dream. It took me
into a beautiful
rainbow, where at the
end of my journey I
was to find my
Forever-Best Friend.
All of a sudden,
I landed
here—next
to you.

"And, WHOooo
are you?" asked Froggie.

"I'm Little Guy.
I, too, have been dreaming, hoping, and
wishing to find a Forever-Best Friend.
A Friend to share with, to be with,
and to have by my side is a gift to
treasure forever."

"Then
kerplunk!
and
here you
are!"

"You know, you look
like the frog from the
carousel over
my bed.
But it can't be.........
How could it be?
How can it be?
But is it?
You?"

"Yes, Little Guy,
I am Froggie."

"Now both our dreams
have surely come true,"
said Froggie.
"We can be as snug as
bugs in a rug and share
the gift of love and
friendship forever."

Froggie and Little Guy held each other tight, both smiling and grinning from left ear to right.
They thanked the fairy princess for guiding them through their paths of dreams, imagination and love;
to find that the "Magic of Friendship" is a gift to treasure no matter who or what that Friend may be.

"Good night, Froggie." "Good night, Little Guy."
ZZZZZZZZZZZZZZZZZZZZZZ

The End

May you be blessed with a
forever-best friend
no matter who or what it may be.